THE ANSWER LIES IN OZ

Detailing the circumstances
of how four fellows who,
by various means
underhanded, fortuitous, and magical,
came to find themselves in the land of Oz

An All-Ages Novella by Charles Shearer

Founded on and continuing
the famous Oz stories by L. Frank Baum

Dedicated to Leah Mickens,
A Musician and a Friend
Who Introduced Me to the Real Oz

The Answer Lies in Oz

Story and Artwork © 2017 by Charles Shearer

Preface by Joe Bongiorno (The Royal Publisher of Oz)

Founded on and continuing the famous Oz stories by L. Frank Baum

https://charlesshearer.info

ISBN 978-0-9984798-1-1
All-ages novella.   FIRST EDITION, 2017   REVISION, 2022

Original text and "This Book Belongs To" illustration: 2008 October in Atlanta, GA
Indicative illustrations and supplemental text: 2016 December in Amherst, NY
Subjunctive illustrations: 2017 June in Amherst, NY
"Upon the Name of Oz" writing: 2017 January, June, and July in Amherst, NY
"Upon the Name of Oz" llustration: 2017 August, November, and December in Amherst, NY

This revision in 2022 January makes slight adjustments to the text and cover, and updates the
status of other works by Charles Shearer.

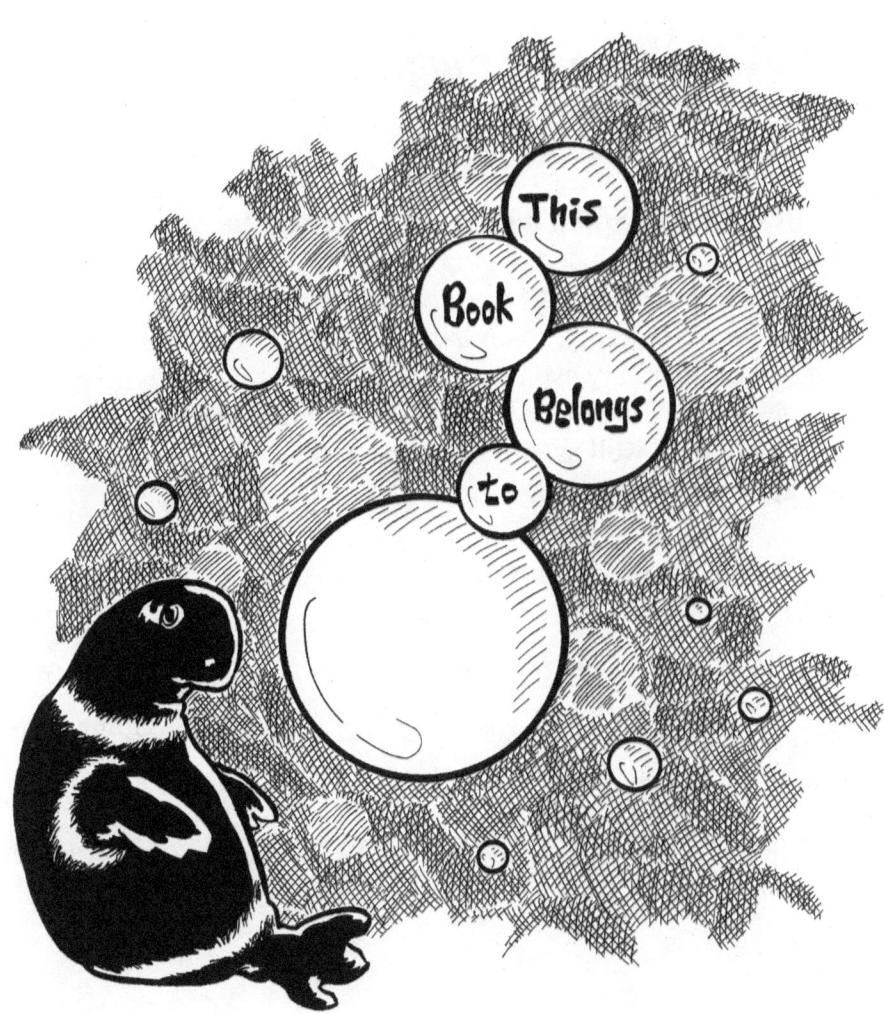

A Few Words from the Author

Being that I wrote *The Answer Lies in Oz* firstly as a gift for a friend who had introduced me to the original Oz of author L. Frank Baum, the intent was to make my story authentic and appropriate in spirit, tone, and continuity. As it is now offered to one and all via this publication, I amend my aspirations for this tale: that it might inspire new interest in the old work of Baum, whose Oz was more fantastical and imaginative, as well as more gruesome, than the enduring array of popular apocrypha based upon it.

Charles Shearer
Amherst, NY
2016 December 16

A Preface from The Royal Publisher of Oz

In the jaded world of publishing, every now and again something unexpected comes along that grabs your attention and holds onto it until long after the story has been read. Charles Shearer's *The Answer Lies in Oz* is one such story. The artwork, initially of the main protagonists, and then of the fantastical environs they travel in, was the first thing that grabbed me and refused to let go. In it were elements of Walt Kelly's *Pogo*, Bill Watterson's *Calvin and Hobbes*, and George Herriman's *Krazy Kat*. Shearer's work isn't an apish imitation of any of these, but his art is redolent of their particular kind of magic. Some will argue, "This is a far cry from John R. Neill," referring to the iconic artist whose illustrations graced most of the canonical Oz books, and they'd be right to a degree. But as anyone who's enjoyed the work of the artists listed above will tell you, there is a kind of realism there; it's deeper in a way too, lying in the nostalgic innocence of Arcadian youth when the days were long and life was full of mystery and possibility.

Yet, *The Answer Lies in Oz* is also arresting in its prose. Some artists can illustrate, but not write; while some can write, but cannot (and should not) illustrate. Shearer is capable of both, and the two complement each other; the story feels like the art; and the art feels like the story; both of which serve to propel the reader into a world that has for over a century been a source of wonder, enigma, joy and enrichment, beginning when L. Frank Baum's iconic *The Wonderful Wizard of Oz* first alighted upon our shores in 1900, spawning not only the first long-running fantasy series, expanded universe, and crossover universe, but the first to feature social commentary. The Oz books showed that fantasy could be more honest, and, therefore, more real than the real world of deceit, obfuscation and subtle manipulation.

Shearer also wisely avoids telling yet another adventure of Dorothy, recognizing that Oz is populated with a vast array of characters who are just as fascinating and entertaining in their own right. Neither does he see the need to re-imagine Oz, a fad from which a few gems have emerged, but which, more often than not, has resulted in a landfill of forgettable, self-indulgent excursions into nowhere. Shearer's Oz is refreshingly the Oz of Baum and his successors, taking place in the outskirts, amongst the strange inhabitants of that land, and serving to enrich by exploration that bizarre realm and our imaginations!

If there's one problem with *The Answer Lies in Oz*, it's that it's too short; but take heart! Shearer has promised me (and, thus, you the reader) that there are more tales to come! I certainly hope so; because now that I've met Eenk, Foof and Quaver, I'm looking forward to spending more time with them as their journey winds throughout the fascinating landscapes and extraordinary peoples that make up the ever-wondrous Land of Oz.

Joe Bongiorno
The Royal Publisher of Oz
www.oztimeline.net

Whom We Shall Meet Herein

Familiar personages in the land of Oz:

Ozma, Princess of Oz — the girlish ruler
The Wizard of Oz — a humbug no longer
The famously wise Scarecrow
Uncle Henry from Kansas

Four new friends from abroad:

Eenk — prickly in demeanor
Foof — prickly in a literal sense
Quaver the musician
The Seal — a seal

List of Chapters

1	A Neighborly Visit	11
2	A Borrowed Vehicle	17
3	A Journey Begun	23
4	A Telling Orchard	28
5	A Strange Desert	34
6	A River Underground	41
7	A New Companion	49
8	A Captain Unconvinced	54
9	A Request Granted	60
10	A Scarf Returned	66
11	A New Country	70
12	A Party Downsized	75
13	A Destination Arrived	84
14	A Musical Performance	94
15	A Gift Giving	99
16	A Learned Council	107
17	A Chosen Itinerary	112
18	An Epilogue	116

1

A Neighborly Visit

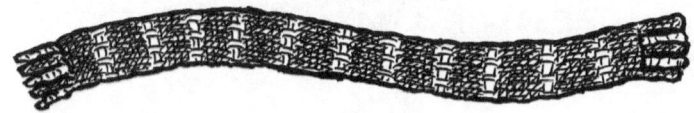

Eenk had a problem, and it was not that he could be a rather cantankerous fellow whom few others could tolerate. That was not the problem, for he was fine with that.

Rather, his problem was something entirely different: no matter how hard he tried, he could not get his trees to bear fruit at all. This was made all the worse by the fact that his neighbors' trees had always done well, and continued to do so, at the time our story took place.

"I can not help but wonder," Eenk said to himself one day, while he was poking and prodding around his uneventful orchard, "if there is not some deliberate mischief at the root of this problem. A gruesome poison planted into the soil, perhaps?"

But he quickly dismissed this notion, as he was often covered with a thin layer of the local dirt and had never noticed any ill effects from it.

"A malevolent incantation, then?" he wondered further, "Some kind of horticultural hex? What competitor, though, is there nearby who would cast a magical disadvantage upon my trees? Not any that I know."

~ ~ ~

Finally, in desperation, Eenk decided to visit one of his neighbors for advice, though it pained him to suffer the presence of another person, for Eenk lived quite alone and liked it that way, if it may be said that he liked anything at all.

To further describe Eenk, while we wait for him to pick a direction in which to walk, it can be said that he was not a tall fellow, nor a tactful one, nor even a well-groomed one, for he did not particularly give a pin what anyone else thought of him, nor did he give much regard to himself. Eenk was very rodent-like in appearance, and accordingly was sometimes prone to nibble on things.

He was walking toward the house of his nearest neighbor, and it had been so long since the two of them had met, that the neighbor's name was not immediately coming to Eenk's mind. But as Eenk was not a tactful creature, this lapse of memory did not bother him in the least.

Upon arriving at the neighbor's house, which was surrounded by fruit-bearing trees, Eenk knocked upon the front door of said house, and it was shortly answered by a tallish person. We might call this neighbor, who was named Foof, tallish only because he was noticeably more tallish than Eenk, but you or I would still be reluctant to call either of them much more than just shortish. Foof was known to have a wide, blank grin, and to-day was no exception. His skin was fuzzy like a peach, but the hairs were as sharp as splinters, and though he had no arms, he did wear a rather fetching scarf and sturdy galoshes, so was therefore not aesthetically lacking. All in all, he looked ready for the winter, and therefore out of place, because it was currently a picturesque morning in the springtime.

"You must know something about trees," Eenk said to him, "as yours currently have a healthy harvest. So tell me why my own will not bear fruit, despite all my best efforts."

"Is it not some toxic presence in the soil?" Foof speculated. "Or a curse placed upon it?"

Eenk groaned.

"I have already considered those explanations, on my own!" he snapped.

Foof thought for a minute or longer, and then said: "Then I'm afraid I don't know, Eenk."

At that point, Eenk would have walked away, but then he might have had to walk even further, to find another neighbor, so he decided to save himself the footsteps and question Foof further.

"If you have no hypothesis which I myself can not imagine,

then who can be of use in advising me on this matter?" asked Eenk.

"I have heard," answered Foof, "that in the far away land of Oz, which is even more of a fairyland than our country, there are wise and magical people who can do many wonderful things. Perhaps you could make a visit there."

"I have never heard of the land of Oz," said Eenk. "Surely there are people more close by who can help!"

"Surely," Foof replied, "but not so much as the great people of Oz."

"Well then," demanded Eenk, "since you know so much about that country, tell me how to get there."

Foof thought for a minute, then gravely responded: "a Deadly Desert lies all around the land of Oz, and no-one can cross it on foot. If anyone tried, that person would turn into dust and be blown away."

"That is alright for you," Eenk said to his neighbor, "for I see that you walk on galoshes, rather than on foot, and therefore could carry me over the sand."

For the first time in the course of this conversation, Foof's blank grin turned into a slight frown, for he knew that his own closest neighbor, Eenk, really did not know him.

"I have no arms to carry you," Foof lamented, "and you could not ride upon me, for my hairs are sharp and would stab you like one thousand splinters!"

"Then some sort of vehicle is called for," Eenk mused.

Foof replied: "In that case, I know someone who can help."

2

A Borrowed Vehicle

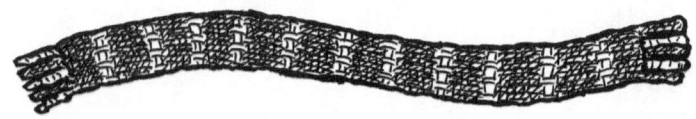

The two neighbors were now walking together, further down the path that connected the different houses of the neighborhood. But to be more accurate, Eenk was walking ahead of Foof, being impatient for a solution, though Foof was rightfully the navigator of this trek, as he was the one among them who knew where their immediate destination was.

After a time, they came upon a ramshackle hut with an equally ramshackle shed attached to it. In the orchard attached to these structures were only a few trees. Though they appeared wild and neglected, they bore healthy fruit.

"Oh, I'd forgotten," said Foof. "It won't do us any good to knock on this front door, just now."

"Why is that?" asked Eenk, to which Foof replied: "Because this is the house of a musician named Quaver. He is not particularly famous in this secluded part of our country, but in other lands, he is apparently very well known for his talents. But we must not bother him now, because he is always asleep during the daytime, and awake at night. It is a habit of exceptional individuals to not do things in normal ways."

Irritated, Eenk fussed and griped, but Foof continued: "I have never actually seen him before, but I have, a few times, happened to walk past here at night, and heard, wafting out from the holes in his house, sonorous rotundity the likes of which I can not adequately describe."

"That bad, eh?" Eenk asked.

At that moment, Eenk and Foof both heard a sonorous rotundity issue forth from inside the hut, but they were both able to confidently identify it as nothing more than snoring.

"But then where is this vehicle you mentioned?" Eenk demanded.

"It's in the shed," Foof simply replied, at which point Eenk stormed to it and unceremoniously opened its door. There, the sunlight fell upon what looked like a small boat, with its bow facing him.

"A boat?!" Eenk exclaimed. "What can I do with a boat, with no water around?!"

Foof stepped forward and explained: "It is not only a boat, Eenk. One night, when I walked by and heard music playing from inside the hut, I saw the vehicle out in the open, and it had four wheels on it."

Sure enough, Eenk then peered inside the small boat, and saw four wheels among the items upon its deck. Feeling better about this vehicle, he pulled out the four wheels and attached them to the outside of the hull, where there were already pegs installed for this purpose, and then pulled the entire vehicle out of the shed, by the bow.

In full sunlight, Eenk could see words engraved on the wheels.

"A circle of fifths," he read from one of the wheels, completely puzzled. "Certainly a wheel is a kind of circle, but there are only four of them! This won't do, at all!"

But as he started to push the vehicle back into the shed in reverse, he noticed, to his amazement, that the engraved words on the wheels had changed.

He read aloud: "A circle of fourths!"

"Musical magic?" Foof wondered aloud.

"This makes much more sense, now," Eenk exclaimed, "but it looks like I'll have to ride this contraption in reverse, or else this poor thing will not know how many wheels it has, and being so confused, might lead me astray."

Foof looked anxious, and asked: "You mean that you're going to ride it? But you can't ask Quaver's permission right now, for he is asleep."

Eenk became irritated at this, but was not discouraged even in the slightest.

"You told me that this musician fellow is asleep during the daytime," he said, "and as it is still morning, he will not wake up for quite some time, and if the supposed land of Oz is far from our own country, then a round trip will take a great while, thus I might as well make imminent departure. Furthermore, look at the state of this hut and shed! They have apparently received no care for quite some time, so perhaps this Quaver fellow is not one to come outside at night, either."

Pausing here, to let his overwhelming logic settle into Foof's mind, Eenk then concluded: "Therefore, I might borrow this vehicle for a span of several days, and by the time the musician ever realizes what's happened, my orchard will be the envy of him, and you, and everyone else, for that matter! ...and I suppose his boat will be returned by then, as well."

Foof thought this plan questionable, for it certainly was, and would have said so, but he knew that Eenk could not be persuaded so easily.

Eenk turned the vehicle around, so that its stern was facing away from the shed, and hopped into the hull. There was only a small deck, to speak of, for it was a small boat, and left lying upon this deck were several items that may or may not have been related to sailing; Eenk could not really tell. But he was more concerned with how this vehicle operates on land, than with how it does on water.

Searching among the items on deck, he found a steering wheel, and then attached it to a peg on the bow. He then found a speed lever among the other items, and attached it to a hole on the bow, below the steering wheel. But he realized that if he were to operate the steering wheel and the speed lever himself, he would have to drive facing the bow, as would normally be proper, but would in this case confuse the four wheels into thinking that they were fifths, instead of fourths. But still, he was not discouraged.

"Neighbor," he said to Foof, because he still did not remember his splintery neighbor's name, "since you are the one who knows the way to Oz, I have appointed you first mate, so that you may steer. I, meanwhile, shall be the captain, and face where we are going, as to not crash into anything."

"You mean for me to go with you?" Foof asked. "I think I could perhaps direct you to the land of Oz, but first let us wait until night, so that we may ask Quaver's permission to borrow the boat."

"If we wait until night," Eenk replied, "then we, ourselves, should be asleep, and will be in no position to make a journey. Besides, if you do not come with me, the wheels will be confused again and might never take me to Oz, nor bring the boat back here to Quaver at all, and he might become quite angry with you."

This put Foof into a tricky position, but after thinking it over for a one or two minutes, he reasoned that it would be best for him to contain the damage by accompanying Captain Eenk on the journey, as first mate.

"Very well," Foof reluctantly replied, climbing into the boat with much difficulty, for we must remember that Foof had no arms. Eenk might have assisted him in this, if not for remembering Foof's sharp hairs.

3

A Journey Begun

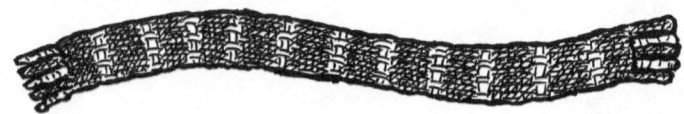

So with Eenk as self-appointed captain and Foof as reluctantly-accepting first mate, the two were ready to begin their trip to the land of Oz. Eenk faced the stern, because he intended the boat to be driven in reverse, and Foof faced the opposite way, to manipulate the controls with his mouth and galoshes-clad feet.

(This is indeed, dear reader, a ridiculous and convoluted situation, is it not? For your consideration, I have left the final page of this book blank, so that you might take some notes and draw a diagram.)

As this was a cumbersome way to operate sensitive controls, as soon as Eenk gave the first order to move the vehicle, Foof nearly crashed the boat into Quaver's hut, which surely would have awoken the musician. So the two adventurers both resolved to be more careful, and the boat awkwardly steered away from the house and the shed.

"Now I am almost completely convinced that this is a magical boat," Eenk said mostly to himself, for though he needed Foof to drive the boat, he did not enjoy the neighbor's presence, and was pleased to not have to look at him, for the time being.

The boat moved along at a brisk pace, out into the open, and which point Eenk directed to Foof: "Steer us towards the land of Oz!"

Foof did so, or at least thought that he did so, for I might as well inform you that Foof was not entirely sure of the correct direction, but at least he had a better idea than the captain did. So the boat drove onward over the ground, through a field, and approached another orchard that perhaps belonged to some other neighbor.

"Trees ahead!" shouted Captain Eenk. "Starboard!"

But Foof began to steer the vehicle directly toward a tree, rather than away from it, for Eenk had not accounted for the vehicle being directed backwards.

(You might also want to clarify this left/right confusion in your notes and diagram.)

"No, port!" the captain yelled. "Port! Now starboard! Now port again!"

The first mate steered wildly, of course still facing away from where the boat was going, but managed to avoid a direct hit upon any of the trees, which is to say that a few low-hanging branches did not survive unscathed.

~~~

The captain and the first mate rode straight through prairie land for a time, without much further incident.

"So who exactly is there in Oz," Eenk asked, "who might solve my problem for me... at no further payment than the satisfaction of performing a noble deed?"

"Well," replied Foof, removing his face from the steering wheel, "I have heard that there is a very wise man, who happens to be a scarecrow stuffed with straw."

This particularly interested Eenk, but he did not interrupt, lest he fail to hear something even more interesting.

"And there is an old farmer from an even further away country called Kansas," continued the first mate, "who is said to be the best farmer in all the known world."

Even still, the captain did not interrupt.

"There are also a number of very magical people," Foof went on, "who are skilled enough to perform wonderful feats, should natural wisdom and farming fail."

Sensing that Foof's knowledge of Oz's useful denizens had now been spoken in full, Eenk freed himself of the burden of having to pay attention to the first mate.

"Yes," the captain replied, "that all sounds very good, indeed! My orchard shall soon put all others to shame!"

4

A Telling Orchard

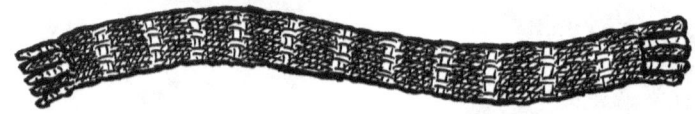

The two of them rode on for quite a while, still at a brisk pace, until they began to approach another orchard. Noticing these trees, the captain became greatly interested, and ordered the first mate to dock at one of them. This task being carried out, Eenk stared at the trees, and at the blossoms growing on their branches.

"These trees look identical to my own," he uttered in awe, "but these blossoms look completely unfamiliar."

"Do they look different from the blossoms on your own trees?" Foof asked.

"I have never seen any blossoms on my own trees," Eenk replied.

"Well," questioned the first mate, "what kind of trees do you have?"

The captain was silent for a moment, then admitted: "I do not know, for I have never seen them bear fruit, by which I may identify the trees."

As the two adventurers spoke, small creatures began to wander toward the boat, tilting their heads in curiosity and waving their hands in greeting. With a start, Captain Eenk noticed them.

"Egads!" he exclaimed at the first one that he saw. "What are you?"

"I am an Aye," the friendly creature replied.

"And what is an Aye?" asked Eenk.

"Half of an Aye-Aye," replied the Aye.

The other Ayes simply nodded their heads in agreement with this exhaustive explanation from one of their own.

"Aye, that is right," said another Aye.

"My name is Anye Wichizwyde," said a thickly-set one to the captain.

"An Aye Which Is Wide?" replied Eenk. "You can not expect me to remember such a long name. I shall call you 'Wyde' for short."

To the captain, a thin Aye said: "My name is Anye Wichiztyte," to whom the captain replied, "Then, An Aye Which Is Tight, I shall call you 'Tyght' for short."

"I don't believe you will!" cried another Aye to Eenk.

The captain addressed this Aye, asking: "Who are you?"

"I am Anye Indenyle," this Aye replied.

"An Aye In Denial?" Eenk said. "Then 'In Denyle' is what I shall declare you, for that is what you are."

Finally, Foof spoke: "Goodness, I hope there is no Anye Onfyre around here!"

"Not this season," replied a local named Anye Forstyle.

More and more Ayes tried to introduce themselves, until Eenk became overwhelmed.

"That's enough!" he cried. "I do not care to know so many folks at once! Now tell me what kind of tree it is that grows in this orchard."

An Aye Which Is Wide replied to him, "It is the Mellilla Tree, which bears the sweetest fruit in the world."

"And how do you Ayes grow these trees so well?" Captain Eenk asked them.

"Oh," An Aye Which Is Tight replied, "we do nothing at all. They just grow by themselves."

"Not true!" cried An Aye In Denial.

Eenk was not satisfied with this answer, but did not think that he could get a better one out of these creatures. Even still, he was not discouraged, for he now knew what kind of tree it is that grows in his own orchard, and what the trees are called. He thought this bit of information would be necessary for him to supply to the learned people of Oz, so that they might properly advise him.

In the meantime, however, he had reached a conclusion of his own: he was thoroughly sick of this place.

Addressing the first mate, Captain Eenk cried: "Onward to Oz!"

At once, First Mate Foof caused the boat to continue its path through the orchard of the Ayes, nearly crashing into a few trees, as well as a few Ayes. Foof would have apologized to the creatures, but his face was busy manipulating the steering wheel, and he therefore could neither see nor speak very well.

~ ~ ~

Shortly, the boat was clear of the orchard, and moving through more prairie land.

"It is just too bad that none of the Mellilla Trees had any fruit, at the moment," Eenk said to himself, "for I would have liked to finally taste one, or to at least see how they look."

Once Foof had steadied the direction and speed of the vehicle, he was able to free up his face and feet.

"The Ayes are interesting, are they not?" he said. "They seem to bear somewhat of a resemblance to you, Eenk, if I may say so."

"No," the captain replied, "you may not."

"But considering that they are of a land very near our own," Foof continued, "and even grow the same type of tree that you... try to... they might be distant relations of yours."

"And perhaps your scarf is a distant relation of yours," Eenk sneered, "for the both of you are raggedy and unsightly."

This hurtful remark ended the conversation, and for a time, they rode on, not speaking to each other. Eenk appreciated the peace and quiet, at least to the extent that he could appreciate anything.

5

A Strange Desert

"We should soon be coming upon the Deadly Desert that separates our country from the land of Oz," Foof finally said after a while, with a reasonable degree of confidence.

But the prairie land continued on and on for a long time, with no meaningful change of scenery.

"Not much further," Foof eventually continued, his confidence becoming less reasonable, especially as the firm ground of grass beneath the speeding vehicle began to look a bit soggy.

"First mate," Eenk said to Foof, because he still could not remember the first mate's actual name, "where is this supposed Deadly Desert of which you had been speaking?"

Foof became worried, for he could not account for a desert not yet being visible, and it was Eenk, after all, who was facing where they were going, and was therefore in a much better position to see what was ahead. Quite to the contrary of Foof's assumption, the slightly soggy ground gradually became undeniably muddy as the vehicle moved along, until the terrain was quite wet and became a swamp. This was thenceforth all that Eenk could see ahead.

"How very odd," he sneered. "Though I have never seen a desert, I always imaged them to be very dry, but this one seems to be exceedingly damp."

The ground was indeed so wet that the wheels increasingly lost speed, until the vehicle was practically crawling through deep pools of murky water, until the ground lost what little sense of solid earth that it had left, at which point Eenk and Foof found themselves trapped upon a vehicle that was no longer making any progress at all. They could hear the wheels spinning in vain, under the surface of the water.

This was an appropriate time for Eenk to lose his patience, and he did not fail to do so.

"Perhaps this supposed land of Oz," he seethed at his first mate, "is just as fictional as the Deadly Desert that precedes it!"

Foof was speechless, his usual wide grin replaced by a wide frown.

"And now look at us!" the captain continued, "We're stuck in the water, in this worthless boat...!"

Suddenly, he realized a solution.

"The wheels!" he cried. "This vehicle must become a vessel! Take off the wheels, first mate!"

Very reluctantly and with great difficulty, Foof did as he was told, cumbersomely climbing over the edge and lowering himself into the water, by his mouth, which was clamped onto the boat. Being in this position, he then carefully dropped into the water and floated around the boat, using his feet to remove each wheel, which then floated upon the surface. Eenk contributed to this effort by then reaching down and rescuing each wheel and placing it upon the deck. Foof then had the even more difficult task of climbing back into the boat, made all the more difficult because his sharp hairs prevented the captain from assisting, even if the captain wanted to, which the captain did not.

Finally, Foof was back upon the deck, his fetching scarf now looking quite soggy and dirty. Much to the surprise of both adventurers, they suddenly found that Foof was no longer quite so tallish any more. In fact, he was now just as shortish as Eenk, and they discovered the cause of this: the first mate had lost his galoshes in the water.

"Fraudulence!" the captain cried. "Your galoshes made you a head taller!"

"Well, you try picking fruit from an orchard," Foof sheepishly replied, "with short legs and no arms!"

Angrily the captain replied: "If I had any fruit to pick, I wouldn't be stuck with you in this farcical excursion, in the first place!"

Indeed, now that Foof's secret shortness was no longer much of a secret, Eenk was greatly distracted from his purpose, but seeing the muddy wheels now placed upon the deck, he remembered his circumstances and resolved to make progress in the journey.

"Get this boat moving," he sneered, "unless having neither

arms nor galoshes is suddenly a great hindrance to you.”

There was no reply from the boat, when Foof tried to manipulate the controls with his face again. The vessel simply would not move, save the subtle rocking caused by nothing more than the two adventurers moving on the deck. Eenk looked among the other items there, hitherto neither used nor examined by either of them, and found a canvas sail, folded inside a box. As Eenk was the one among them with hands, he unfolded the sail and examined it.

“How is this sail to work, what with there being no wind in this Damply Desert?” he asked.

“Maybe it works by magic upon the water, like the wheels do upon the land,” Foof timidly replied, still feeling crestfallen by his cantankerous companion.

So Eenk rummaged around amongst the other items lying on the deck, until he found sections of a mast, and when he brought the ends of the sections close together correctly, they joined together into solid pieces, until one entire mast was assembled. He then attached the sail to the mast, and having done this, he now reasoned that an upright sail should take the place of the steering wheel, so he switched out the parts upon the peg.

At once, the boat began to move erratically upon the surface of the water, spinning this way and that way.

“Grab the free end of the sail in your mouth!” the captain commanded.

The first mate obliged, and the boat set out upon a straight path across the water, still going in what would properly be called a reverse direction, relative to the vehicle.

"This steering business is very complicated," Foof could only mumble, as he was holding part of the sail in his teeth. "Now that there are no wheels to get confused, might we start driving the boat forward instead of backward?"

The captain grumbled, but seeing the first mate's logic, agreed, and after the boat had been maneuvered around, it set off in a proper forward direction, continuing the journey.

(You may now erase your notes and diagram.)

~~~

So Foof was now in the front, steering as he pleased, leaving Eenk in the back to do not much of anything but idly pass the time as the boat sailed along.

"I think I should like to meet that scarecrow fellow whom you mentioned," Eenk said.

"Because he is very wise?" Foof asked, still holding an end of the sail in his teeth.

"No," replied Eenk, "because you said he is stuffed with hay, and I would like to give it a good nibble."

"I believe it is straw, and not hay, that you are thinking of," as Foof's reply.

"No," said the captain, "it is indeed hay that I am thinking of, for I am presently quite hungry."

To be truthful, both adventurers were hungry, for they had not eaten since before beginning their journey, having not known that they were to embark upon it until they were about to do so. But as there did not appear to be anything to eat nearby, in the swamp, they had no choice but to continue on.

6

A River Underground

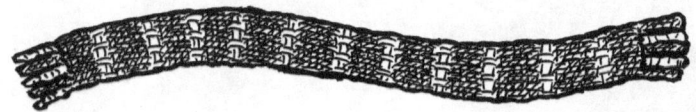

The water became wider and deeper, the further they sailed on. The adventurers now found themselves on a lake that was much more aesthetically pleasing than the swamp.

"A lovely view, wouldn't you agree?" Foof asked, his pronunciation not coming out very elegantly.

Without great enthusiasm, Eenk replied: "This looks even less like a desert than the swamp did."

"But at least on the bright side," Foof continued, "there might be some edibles in the water below."

Eenk was in no mood to look on the bright side.

"Perhaps there are creatures lurking below us," he said, "who are, at this very moment, saying to themselves that there might be some edibles in the boat above."

~~~

The expanse of water before them was vast, and because Foof already had considerable reason to doubt his own navigational skills, he did not know in which direction to sail, and so he kept the vessel going straight ahead.

Barely visible were various communities of hitherto unseen peoples, at several distant points along the wide circumference of the lake.

Before Foof could even make the suggestion that was on his mind, Eenk refused, saying: "We are not asking them for directions. If those folk living along the shoreline are anything alike the ones populating the blooming Mellilla orchard, I would rather not meet them."

~~~

The adventurers' boat sailed onward across the middle of the lake, into an increasingly narrow pathway between two sandy banks. This waterway became a river, its water speeding up, the narrower the path became, until the boat's speed was so great that Foof could hardly manage to hold the end of the sail in his mouth. The river began to slant downward before them, the rushing wind hitting the first mate so hard, that Foof was afraid he could no longer grip the sail. Furthermore, the water began to crash against the increasingly rocky shores, abruptly rocking the boat, and with Foof being so jostled, the sail finally broke free of his grip, and swayed uselessly behind the mast, its magic simply not strong enough to direct the vessel's course any longer.

As the boat was carried onward, the rocky shore rose higher and higher, as if to encompass the river, until a ceiling of rock and earth completed the rocky arch. As the sunlight grew thinner, the adventurers found themselves plunged into darkness amongst the violent waves and rushing wind.

The roar was deafening, and the momentum was such that both adventurers clung to the hull as well as they could, Eenk by his hands and Foof by his teeth, for fear of being thrown from the vessel. But just then, at its worst, the din and the jostling abruptly ceased, and still in darkness, the two adventurers felt as if weightless and unsupported, in a terrifying void.

Just as suddenly as this came on, it ended all at once, with a jarring crash upon cold water. For a few moments, the two adventurers were submerged, but the boat then rose back up upon the surface and flipped over forward. Neither Eenk nor Foof could manage to keep holding on, being so disoriented, and felt themselves drift away from the boat.

But as the rocking and the roar of the water gradually subsided, the two adventurers floated near the surface of the water, surrendering to its power, but also realizing that the worst was over.

True to their belief, they presently washed up on a sandy shore, where finally opening their eyes again, they saw thin shafts of sunlight beaming from above. Wearily standing up and regaining their breath, Eenk and Foof staggered toward the rays of light shining down from holes in the ceiling of the cave in which they found themselves.

Now visible to each other in the light, they both looked to be in sad shape: Eenk was a matted mess of wet fur and sand, but less dirt, while Foof had lost some of his sharp hairs to the raging water, and his once fetching scarf was now missing from around his neck, also taken by the water.

"You had mentioned neither the swamp," Eenk grumbled, "nor the lake, nor the tunnel, nor the waterfall, before we set out."

"I did not know about them," was Foof's reply.

"Yet you did somehow know about the land of Oz," Eenk muttered, "which is supposedly located beyond all of those horrible things. How did you manage such a feat of knowledge?"

"The land of Oz is a famous country," Foof timidly explained. "There are few people who do not know something of its wonders. I suppose that the unwonderful parts do not get mentioned in the stories."

Without another word at this point, Eenk walked back toward the water, to try to discover what had become of the boat and its parts. This underground section of the cave was not as dark as the section just before the waterfall, so by and by, Eenk was able to wrangle together most of what had been lost. The boat itself seemed to be intact, and the wheels had washed up upon the shore, as had the sail, the steering wheel, the speed lever, and most of the sections of the mast, plus a few other items

that neither adventurer had yet used during the journey.

But Foof's scarf was nowhere to be found.

With the boat halfway upon the shore, Eenk loaded everything onto the deck and climbed aboard, but did not re-install anything except the steering wheel, which he grasped firmly with both hands.

Presently, he said to Foof: "This subterranean river has a current of its own, so I will not need the sail. Just push the boat into the water, whether you are coming along or not. But do not think, even for a moment, that I will again trust you to manipulate the controls."

Feeling dejected for the loss of his scarf more than anything else, Foof pushed the boat fully onto the surface of the water, and then laboriously climbed into the boat, by his teeth and bare feet. The poor fellow had lost everything: his galoshes, his scarf, and even some of his sharp hairs, not to mention his sense of direction, apparently. He said nothing as the boat began to drift further down the underground river.

Much in contrast with what came before, this section of the water had only a slight current and a gentle disposition. As the adventurers sailed along, more rays of sunlight came into view, around the cave's curves ahead, and drifted overhead before disappearing behind them. In this way, the sunlight gradually became fuller as the rays became more frequent, and before too long, the interior of the cave was illuminated well enough for Eenk and Foof to plainly see the details of the craggy surfaces around them.

They could even see creatures swimming in the river, though their exact forms remained mysterious, as of yet.

A New Companion

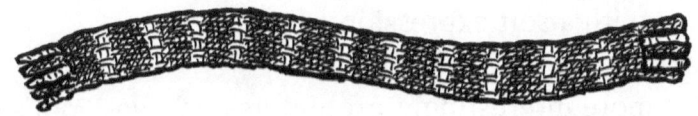

Finally, the river led the still soggy adventurers to the end of the cave, where the rocky walls fully yielded to open sunlight and fresh air. The scenery was pleasant enough, and wild plants grew along the banks.

This reminded both Eenk and Foof of how hungry they were, so after a nod from the captain, the first mate carefully steered the boat to shore, where it came to a rest. Climbing out onto the land, they both foraged around the tall grasses and fruit-bearing bushes, Eenk nibbling on some thin stalks of grain, and Foof taking bites out of the bushes, leaves and all.

Eating in this way, Foof happened to be facing the water, and saw one of the mysterious creatures seen earlier, presently swimming along with the current, carrying a familiar object with it.

"My scarf!" Foof cried in recognition, and at once gave chase.

Running alongside the creature, Foof shouted: "Excuse me! Stop, please!"

Slowing and spiraling to a stylish stop, the creature poked its head and neck out of the water, revealing the form of a sleek, plump seal with a soft expression.

But more interestingly, around its neck was Foof's scarf.

Now attentive, the seal asked: "Yes, what is it?"

"I was hoping you might return my scarf," Foof replied, "which the waterfall took away from me."

"You say this item belonged to you?" the seal then asked, looking down at the scarf.

"It still does," Foof replied, as steadily as he could.

"Oh dear," the seal replied in earnest concern, for he was a considerate fellow, "I thought that it belonged to me, because I found it here in the river, but found no-one attached to it. But I suppose we may share it."

This offer caught Foof off-guard, and after hastily thinking for a few moments, he said: "How might we share it?"

"Let us take turns," the seal proposed. "In this way, we may periodically trade off, so that neither of us might grow accustomed to the item's novelty, too soon."

"But I really can not remain here," Foof said, "for we are on a journey."

"We are?" the seal questioned.

"Yes," Foof answered, "We: my neighbor and I, seek the land of Oz, to ask advice from its learned and magical citizens on an important matter."

~~~

Foof's neighbor, namely Eenk, was meanwhile still near the boat, nibbling on stalks of grain, because he had taken entirely no interest in the matter of Foof chasing after the wet, pitiful scarf. After a few minutes, Eenk noticed Foof walking back, with a scarf-wearing seal swimming alongside him in the water, against the current.

Foof gave Eenk a hopeful, sheepish grin, to which Eenk only gave an annoyed stare in return.

"I've met someone who wants to go with us to Oz," Foof explained. "If we agree to take him there, he will give me back my scarf, and entirely repeal his claim on it."

"Why can he not go to Oz by himself," Eenk asked, "and keep the scarf all for himself, in the process?"

The seal piped in, not realizing that Eenk had not actually been seeking an answer: "Because being a seal, I can not travel well upon the land, and there are no waterways that lead through or under the Deadly Desert, into Oz."

"He can swim alongside our boat," Foof continued, "and when it is time to re-attach the wheels and ride on land, he can ride with us to Oz, at which point I will have my scarf completely returned to me."

"That is all well and good for you two," Eenk scowled, "but what would be the benefit to me, in allowing this third wheel alongside a vessel that is already confused about how many wheels it has?"

Again, the seal piped in: "From a certain vantage point, several forks far down the river, I have countless times seen the edge of the Deadly Desert that completely surrounds the land of Oz, and I can lead you to it. From there, it will be I who will depend upon you, Mister Captain, for kindness and assistance. Does this seem to be a fair agreement, to you?"

Being entirely unfamiliar with anything that might lie ahead, Eenk supposed that he, himself, had only a slim chance of guessing the correct turns to take, if there were indeed forks ahead in the river. Without the seal's guidance, the two original adventurers might easily take a wrong turn in steering the vessel and end up hopelessly lost forever.

"Then I agree," Eenk said.

8

A Captain Unconvinced

So from that point onward, there were three adventurers, instead of just two, on this journey which was no longer nearly so hopeless at it had been. In fact, things were looking quite positive, indeed. The captain even dared to imagine that he just might end up learning the secret to make his trees back home bear fruit.

Eenk and Foof rode in the boat, with the captain steering and the first mate not steering. The seal swam alongside, in the water of the river.

After a good while, the seal pulled out in front, for sure enough, there was indeed a fork ahead. The seal swam toward the left branch, and the boat followed. This subsequent part of the river flowed onward for another good while, along an unwavering curve through a dense forest, which prevented any viewer from seeing very far ahead. But the seal, of course, knew the way through the water, and so he had no concern about what stood outside of the water. He again swam alongside the boat for a while.

Thinking aloud, Eenk remarked: "And here I was half-expecting there to be no forks at all, and that this seal was just tricking us into taking him along."

"Eenk," Foof nervously warned, "you might not want to insinuate such an ill scheme against our new companion, or else he might feel insulted, and then only begrudgingly return complete ownership of my scarf to me."

~ ~ ~

After a few minutes more, a tributary appearing on the starboard side joined with the section of river upon which our three adventurers were traveling, flowing with the same gentle current. This made Captain Eenk suspicious.

(Now that the final page of this book has been freed up, you might start drawing a map.)

"Seal, where does that way come from?" Eenk called out to the seal.

"From danger, Mister Captain," the seal vaguely replied.

Eenk was not at all sure about this new traveling companion, but Foof thought him a decent enough fellow, or was at least hopeful about getting his scarf back.

Another fork soon appeared in the river, and the seal again led them toward the left branch. Following it, the boat continued sailing, still surrounded by forest, until some minutes later, when again another tributary joined back with their own, just as had taken place before.

This renewed Eenk's suspicion.

"Now I am almost certain that this newcomer takes us for a ship of fools," Eenk grumbled to himself. "I'd bet my furry little ears that these supposed forks are just islands in the river, and that each side leads to the same place."

"Please," implored Foof, "we must trust our navigator! He would not lead us astray."

"Who are you to judge his sense of direction!?" snapped the captain. "You do not even possess one of your own! ...a fact that you would have done well to announce to me, at the start!"

Before Foof could reply, he noticed a third fork approaching, and the seal leading them toward the right-side branch, this time. Eenk saw this, but was no longer in any mood to cooperate. Having a mind to test his hypothesis, he steered the boat toward the left branch, leaving the seal to take the right branch alone.

"There," Eenk bellowed, "if we sail further along and find our navigator re-joining us from another one of those tributaries, then we will certainly know him to be fraudulent!"

For a minute or so, their chosen path was as placid as any

other, but soon after that short time had elapsed, the captain and the first mate espied jagged rocks jutting up from the water's surface, ahead. Eenk steered around them, only to inadvertently bump the boat against rocks that were lying barely below the surface. In this way, the boat was jostled against obstacles both obvious and oblique, not quite within the captain's control, and in his frustration, he oversteered, sending the boat spinning until it was progressing sideways, and therefore nigh unsteerable.

"We've gone backward, and then forward, and now sideways!" cried Foof. "This is terribly inconsistent!"

Bumping against a few more rocks before Eenk was able to orient the bow forward again, the river presently calmed down and was joined by another tributary, and as the suspicious captain had anticipated, it was in this way that the seal re-joined them.

"You, seal!" Eenk called out, upon which point the seal poked his head above the water's surface and stared, as if startled at being addressed in such a way.

"Yes, what is it?" the seal asked, regaining his grace and composure.

"All those three forks lead to this same place, don't they?!" Eenk bellowed. "You've led us nowhere that we could not have found ourselves!"

"But you did not know which ways were free of danger," the seal indicated, and then fully sank back into the water and swam onward.

If Eenk had been the type of fellow to feel shame and embarrassment, which he was not, then he would have felt those emotions at that moment. But futile irritation was a state known to him, and it was this emotion that he did feel, instead.

After a while more of the boat sailing and the seal swimming, respectively, the forest that had hitherto surrounded the river gradually thinned out, leaving unsightly savanna bordering the water. As desolate as this was, what next came into view, shortly off the starboard side, made the sparse grassland look thriving and radiant, by comparison: a vast expanse of nothing but shifting sand and glaring sunlight.

The seal pulled up along the riverbank and rested with his two front flippers upon the thin layer of remaining savanna, and said: "There before us is the Deadly Desert."

9

A Request Granted

The boat moored upon the edge of the savanna, where it met the water. Eenk and Foof climbed out, and feeling the roughly exposed earth and dying grasses underfoot, gazed with squinting eyes into the seemingly unending stretch of desert. Nothing at all could be seen where it met the horizon, save the waving of oppressive heat.

"We must be careful not to step much closer," Foof warned, "for the tales say that anyone who sets foot upon the sand of the Deadly Desert is turned into dust and blown away, and I no longer even have my galoshes."

"I have seen such a thing happen," the seal verified. "Many of my kind have longed to venture to Oz, but none have made it past even one flipper-print upon the sand, before falling victim to

it. How lamentable!"

Eenk gave the seal a frustrated look, and questioned: "Why would any seal wish to go to the land of Oz?"

"Because," the seal explained, "it is the earnest wish of every one of my kind to walk as freely upon the land as freely we swim in the water, but our natural form only permits us to crawl or scamper upon terra firma. We have heard that in the land of Oz, there live powerful practitioners of magic, who could allow us to fulfill our wish, by means of some spell or artifact, if only we could first find a way to reach the people of that country. Just to-day, you two travelers happened by in a boat that the first mate assured me can also travel upon the land, and in this way, I might be the first of my kind to venture to Oz!"

"If we maintain enough speed," Foof proposed, "the vehicle should be able to stay upon the surface of the sand, keeping us alive. It would not be the first time that a person has crossed the Deadly Desert by speeding upon its length, in a single effort."

Eenk made no reply to this, but instead began to attach the wheels to the boat. As the boat was still oriented with the bow facing forward, the wheel nearest to Eenk bore the words "a circle of fifths," which irritated him. So he turned the boat around, so that its stern was facing the Deadly Desert and its wheels would therefore not be confused as to how many there were.

But Eenk noticed that one of the wheels did not bear the words "a circle of fourths," as the others did, but rather: "a major third."

He was truly dismayed at this, but was too weary to grumble at tremendous volume.

"Now only three of the wheels know how many there are," Eenk muttered, "and one of them thinks that there are only three! I shall certainly have more than a few words with Quaver the musician about these hopelessly confounded devices of his, if I ever get the chance."

~~~

Now that the vessel was again a vehicle and was properly oriented and equipped for travel upon land, Eenk was about to climb aboard, when the seal once again piped up: "What about the water?"

"We just left the water," Eenk replied.

So the seal explained: "I mean the water that you'll have to keep in the land-boat for me, so that I'll stay wet and healthy."

Eenk stared at the seal for a full minute, in utter silence.

This made poor Foof fear that the plan was going awry, now at this critical phase, for he would not wholly get his scarf back without first safely escorting the seal to Oz.

"Please, Eenk," Foof pleaded, "he is a seal, after all!"

Hearing this, Eenk turned away from the both of them, and said: "Then get to it."

So while Eenk sat down and waited, and the arm-less Foof could only stand by and watch, the seal began splashing water up into the vehicle. Understandably, this took a while, for there was no bucket available for the task, and the seal could not have used one, even if one had been available.

"This flippered fellow will manage to sink a boat... upon the land!" Eenk muttered.

~~~

Finally, when the task was reasonably completed, the three adventurers climbed into the vehicle. Eenk, wishing to face the intended direction of travel, stood at the stern, leaving Foof to manipulate the controls at the bow, as had been the case amongst the orchards and on the prairies.

(Consult your old notes and diagram, of which you were likely too proud to erase.)

Meanwhile, the seal waded in the water that he had so laboriously splashed up. He was situated between the captain and the first mate, who could not help but stand in the water, as there was nowhere else available. In such close proximity, the seal would need to be especially wary of Foof's needle-sharp hairs.

"Forward!" cried Captain Eenk.

"You mean 'backward,' do you not?" Foof sheepishly replied.

Thusly, the vehicle began to move past the thin layer of savanna, and onto the burning sand of the Deadly Desert.

10

A Scarf Returned

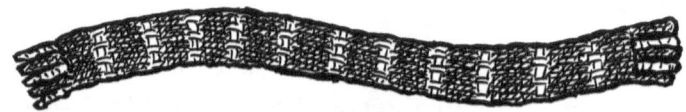

As speedily as it could go, the vehicle carried Eenk, Foof, and the seal through the desert. The sand gently yielded under the three circles of fourths and the one major third, somewhat slowing them down, from lack of optimal traction.

The vehicle traveled onward for some time, but still, there was nothing but desert visible ahead, and the intense heat and sunlight were beginning to wear down the three adventurers. The seal was doing his best to lay flat in the layer of water, so that he could stay as wet as possible. This was difficult, for the seal was noticeably plump, and the heat of the Deadly Desert was so intense that the water's gradual evaporation was undeniable.

Eenk and Foof, meanwhile, had to be content with just their legs being soaked, for the time being, as they tried to shield their eyes from the harsh sunlight.

On and on, for a long time, nothing but desert could be seen lying before them. Conditions were so bad that Foof could not even bother to think about his scarf, still being worn by the seal. Another long time passed, and still, all was the same, the harsh desert air whipping past them as the vehicle traveled at its maximum speed possible.

The captain and the first mate's ankles were even starting to dry. With such a low water level, by this point, the poor seal was especially at the mercy of the Deadly Desert.

~~~

But then, it was as if the vehicle had penetrated some invisible barrier, for all at once, the adventurers found themselves speeding upon lush hills of purple grass, amidst trees with purple leaves, and the entire presence of the Deadly Desert had completely vanished. With the speed lever still set at the maximum, and the land now being much firmer, the vehicle had greatly increased in speed.

Just as Eenk was on the very point of yelling for the first mate to stop the vehicle, he realized that too abrupt a deceleration would hurl all three of them into the air, causing any manner of injury or discomfort. So being of his particular nature, Eenk lunged toward the speed lever, and gripping it tightly, moved it into the "stop" position. In this way, he would remained attached to the vehicle, and only the other two adventurers would be ejected from it.

Thus, Foof and the seal kept moving though the vehicle did not, and presently found themselves landing upon the purple grass in several unceremonious crashes and rebounds, along with the shallow depth of unevaporated water, which splashed over not a very large area. When Eenk, relatively unjostled by his own coming to a stop, looked out toward his companions, he saw them splayed out at some distance.

"Were I not such a quick thinker," Eenk said to himself,

"something bad might have happened."

Foof and the seal groggily oriented themselves and realized what had happened, and gave displeased glares in the captain's direction, but were too sore to pay him such regard for very long. Taking a minute to rest, Foof and the seal only then realized that the scarf was no longer being worn by the seal. They both looked around, and then saw it lying upon the purple grass, some distance away.

Foof and the seal then looked at each other for a moment.

"Mister First Mate," the seal said, "I relinquish my stake of ownership over the scarf, for I had promised you full possession of the item in question, in exchange for bringing me to the land of Oz."

"Is this Oz?" Foof asked, still dazed.

"I assume so," the seal replied.

"Then I thank you," the first mate said.

Foof unsteadily stood up, and walking to the scarf, picked it up with his teeth and twirled it around himself, until it was finally worn around his neck, once again, though a bit soggy.

11

A New Country

When all three adventurers were back in the vehicle, they began to travel through this strange purple country at an easy pace, going over gentle hills of purple grass, until little purple houses could be seen. As there were several people milling about amongst the houses, Eenk ordered the vehicle stopped, so that he might ask a few questions of the locals. These people in question were all neatly dressed in purple costumes, the likes of which none of the three adventurers had ever seen.

"Tell me," Eenk asked one of the purple-clad people, "what country is this?"

"Can you not see the abundance of purple?" the fellow replied. "This is the Gillikin country, of course!"

Shocked, Eenk turned to Foof and the seal, howling: "But you two said that we would be in Oz!"

"Well then," the seal frowned at Foof, "I suppose we shall still have to share the scarf, after all."

The purple-clad fellow chuckled, and explained: "Why, the Gillikin country is a part of the land of Oz!"

"Is it, then?" Eenk replied, now interested. "Then where are the famous learned people and magicians?"

"I would expect them to be concentrated in the Emerald City," was the reply.

"And how do we get there?" the captain inquired.

Indeed, the three adventurers truly were strangers here. Even you or I could have offered a decent answer to Eenk's question.

The local fellow pointed in some direction, and said: "Keep going east, until you come to the Yellow Brick Road, at which point you would want to follow it, going south. It will take you all the way to the Emerald City."

Being the type that felt no need to thank the local fellow, Eenk ordered the vehicle driven onward again, leaving the cluster of purple houses behind.

Now having a direction to follow and a little more specific information, the adventurers took some time to relax, while touring the countryside of the Gillikin country. This part of their journey was the easiest, and sported the best scenery. As their speed was not excessive, they did not cover any impressive distance before the day began to grow late.

"This has been the longest day that I have ever experienced," Foof thought aloud, "and I think I shall certainly appreciate tonight's rest."

~~~

Just as the sun was setting, the three adventurers came upon another cluster of purple houses. There were lights glowing in the windows. Eenk ordered the vehicle parked amidst a few trees, and the three of them lowered themselves down to the grassy ground.

"What is to be done in regard to our sleeping arrangements?" the seal asked.

"I suppose we had better ask some of the locals for lodging," Foof replied.

Dismissing this idea, Eenk said: "I will leave you both to such an idea, for to-day I have been far too crowded with the presence of others, and I certainly do not wish to spend the night in a similar fashion."

Finished speaking, he carefully tilted the vehicle over until it was upside down, and then crawled underneath. There was some degree of privacy and enough room for him to lie down there. Presently, he resolved to ignore the other two adventurers

and to go to sleep.

So Foof and the seal made their way toward the cluster of houses.

"You see what difficulty a seal has upon land," the seal pointed out, as he could only hop and scamper, rather than actually walk. "But soon, I will be magicked a way to freely walk, and even run and jump, if I so please."

"But what if having two legs meant you could no longer swim?" Foof asked.

This startled the seal, for he had not considered this, before.

"Oh my," he said. "When I am petitioning whatever wizard or sorcerer I may end up finding, I shall have to consider that point, for a seal that can no longer swim ceases to be a seal, at all."

12

A Party Downsized

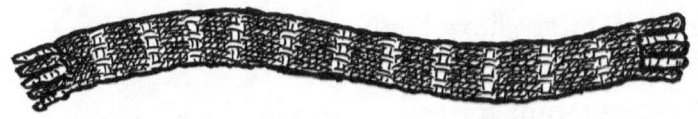

When Eenk awoke the next morning, he crawled out from underneath the overturned vehicle. Foof and the seal were nowhere to be seen, which did not particularly concern Eenk, or to be more accurate, it did not concern him at all. Being of a single-mindedness, Eenk was determined to continue on the journey, and so he set the vehicle upright and climbed aboard.

"Oh," he realized, "if I leave without the other two, I'll have to manipulate the controls, myself, and I can hardly do so for any great distance, if continuing to drive backward."

This irritated him, but he did reluctantly climb back down from the vehicle and turn it around, so that the bow was facing forward, as would normally be proper for a boat. Accordingly, the wording on the wheels now changed: three of them now each read "A circle of fifths," but one read "A tritone."

"Indeed, Quaver shall get a two earfuls about these wheels!" Eenk muttered, "But for now, I can only hope they do not lead me astray, despite the fact that they are even more confused than ever, what with three of them thinking there are five, and one still thinking there are only three."

Without further delay, he himself drove the vehicle onward, leaving the cluster of houses behind, as well as Foof and the seal, wherever they might have been.

We might think the captain unkind for so readily abandoning his mates, but let us not judge him too harshly, for he neither concerned himself with their subsequent travel arrangements nor harbored ill will toward them. So, the matter being adequately described, let us rejoin the narrative.

Though now having no choice but to manipulate the vehicle's controls by himself was of some annoyance to him, Eenk did appreciate traveling alone, if it may be said that he could appreciate anything.

He was now driving through a purple forest that was growing increasingly dense, to the point that branches of purple leaves were hitting him about the face and torso as he rode past. In fact, it seemed to him that the branches were doing so on purpose, and indeed, they began to swing and swoop unnaturally toward him.

In defense, he crouched as low as was possible to still see where he was going, with his hands rising up to cover himself, when the steering wheel or the speed lever did not require his input.

At last emerging through the unfriendly forest, he rode over ground where the grass became increasingly taller, almost as if noticeably growing in his presence. This considerably impeded the vehicle's progress.

But worse yet, interspersed amongst the tall blades of grass were even taller weeds, and as Eenk approached them, their blooms burst apart into clouds of wafting debris. As such, Eenk had to navigate with his eyes closed, coughing and sneezing uncontrollably. This took what seemed like quite a while, being that the plants had slowed the vehicle's progress.

Finally past this ordeal, but with debris still stuck in his fur, Eenk drove over hills of short grass, picking up speed.

But then he met with one more hindrance to his journey: just ahead, there appeared a gorge that stretched as far left and right as was visible, over which there was a single wooden bridge, but the bridge was obviously broken. In fact, the middle section of it was completely missing, and to attempt to drive over it would surely result in the vehicle falling into the gorge below.

Seeing this, Eenk slowed the vehicle to a stop, and considered what he might do. There was no slant that might allow the vehicle to propel itself over the hole, nor were there any other bridges visible.

"The vehicle will never get across that gap," he said to himself.

But then he noticed, just barely, that far across the gorge, there was something visible that appeared long and yellow.

"Could that be the famed Yellow Brick Road?" he wondered aloud, and then muttered: "I'm almost there, and once I reach it, at least the rest of the way to the Emerald City will be obvious, regardless of the distance to it."

Thus, he got an idea.

Steadying himself to carry it out, he at once brought the vehicle up to its maximum speed, heading straight for the broken bridge. Unwavering, he rode out upon the still intact planks, until the three circles of fifths and the one tritone were now treading upon nothing but air, and the vehicle began to fall with the force of gravity, still being propelled forward. At the last moment, Eenk leapt out with all his strength...!

...and landed roughly upon the other side of the broken bridge, having cleared the gap.

We must assume that the poor boat continued its descent, but by the time Eenk regained his footing, the lost vehicle was now gone from his mind, and he continued onward without it. If we, ourselves, were to peer into the gorge at that time, we would see nothing but descending darkness.

Eenk was now quite alone, which was agreeable to his nature. Before him was an expanse of rolling purple hills, with what appeared to be the Yellow Brick Road at the end of it.

For a long time, Eenk walked onward with his stubby legs,

which he found to be quite a tiring ordeal. He had never walked so far, at once, but his traveling on foot was only just beginning.

At last, he reached what was indeed the Yellow Brick Road, and followed it toward his right side, which was toward the south.

The road led him through forests, and plains, and hills, and valleys, for so long that when night was nearly upon him, the Emerald City was still not within sight. Exhausted from walking all day, as well as from hunger, for there was nothing to eat except the ubiquitous purple grass, he thought he might sleep, and resume his walking in the morning.

He laid himself down beneath a tree, right next to the road, and was soon asleep.

~~~

After waking up the next morning, he spent the entire day walking down the Yellow Brick Road, stopping every so often to unsuccessfully forage for food. He did not even see any houses or noticeable dwellings of any kind, the entire day.

When the sun began to set, he again fell asleep beneath a tree, terribly hungry, with nibbling on his mind.

~~~

On the third day of tedious walking, his mind became unhinged.

Perhaps it was all the tiresome traveling on foot, or the lack of suitable food to eat, or the fact that he was basically lost in a foreign land under the presence of yet another sunset, but whatever the reason, thoughts of hopelessness and discouragement began to take root in his mind. They began as an inkling, then grew to a suspicion, then swelled to a nagging worry, until it consumed him, and he stumbled about, gnashing his teeth together.

He fell to his knees and began to nibble the yellow bricks of the road beneath him, but they were too hard and hurt his teeth.

Realizing that in this most desperate time in all his life, he could not even nibble, he futilely laid himself down upon the Yellow Brick Road and stayed there, staring blankly upward at the sky.

"I fear I shall die here, on this spot," he thought aloud, "and for what? Just to make my trees... my Mellilla trees... bear fruit!? What good shall the sweetest fruit in all the world do for me, when I am far away, and also dead?"

Then he thought for a minute or more, and slowly, something new entered his mind.

"And I did bring those other two along, to suffer a similar fate," he muttered. "I suppose that was not quite right."

Having spoken these words, Eenk closed his eyes.

He then experienced a strange sensation, or rather, a moment of utterly no sensation. He thought that it must be death coming to claim him.

When his senses returned, it was not the Yellow Brick Road that he felt beneath him.

When he opened his eyes, it was not the sky that he saw above him.

Rather, what he did feel and he did see were beyond his powers of comprehension.

13

A Destination Arrived

Above Eenk was a high dome of marble, decorated with patterns of emeralds that glowed beautifully from the sunlight coming in through rows of arched windows. Sitting up in astonishment, he realized that he was quite alone in this massive room, which was only lighted by the just mentioned windows within the dome.

The floor and walls were very dark, but then a door opened before him, at which point gentle light revealed the form of someone remarkably tallish entering the room.

From this personage emerged a voice most melodious: "That was hardly any kind of an apology for your selfishness, but it will do."

Slowly, the room became lighter all throughout, letting the forms of the arcaded walls and ornate marble floor be plainly seen.

But even more stunning was the now quite conspicuous figure of a beautiful young lady, wearing a golden crown upon a head of cascading hair, which framed a face even more beautiful. From her shoulders hung flowing garments that were encircled by a large belt, and in her hands she carried a scepter of diamonds and ivory.

Such a sight Eenk never could have imagined, and even now, he could not believe what he was beholding.

"I died!" Eenk cried.

"No, Eenk," said the girl. "You are quite alive."

"How do you know my name?" he asked.

"I know your name, because I had been watching you and your companions from afar, for some time. Now I will tell you my own name: I am Ozma, ruler of the land of Oz. You are now within my palace inside the middle of the Emerald City."

Eenk was, understandably, in dumbstruck awe over hearing this. The overwhelming evidence upon his senses left him no room for doubting the truth of what Ozma said, and there was something about her voice and appearance and demeanor that inspired utter trust from him.

What he could not imagine was how all of this could be

possible.

"Come walk with me," Ozma said, as if reading his mind, "and all shall be explained to you."

Presently, Eenk and Ozma were walking down a hallway. The two of them were quite in contrast: Eenk, shabby and looking quite pathetic, as well as being hungrier than he had ever been, was walking alongside the superbly regal and exquisitely adorned Princess of Oz.

"Your companions are waiting for you," Ozma said.

This caused Eenk a bit of anxiety, for he feared they might be upset with him.

As if reading his mind again, Ozma said: "Do not worry. They have been comfortably situated within the palace for nearly three days, so neither Foof nor the seal are terribly upset with you, any more."

"Foof!" Eenk cried. "So that is his name?"

~~~

Ozma and Eenk arrived at a particular door, which Ozma opened, revealing a lavishly furnished room. Inside were Foof lounging upon a wooden couch that could not be damaged by his spines, and the seal floating in a porcelain tub filled with water.

Both of them were currently enjoying a meal, the sight of which reminded Eenk of his own terrible hunger. To one side of them was a table laid out with a small bale of hay upon a silver tray, and knowing it was meant for himself, Eenk rushed toward it, to satiate his appetite. He paid no attention to the companions he had abandoned back in the Gillikin countryside, until he had chewed and nibbled all the hay that he could handle.

Thus satisfied, he finally noticed that in one corner of the room was the vehicle that he thought had been lost to the gorge with the broken bridge. It appeared quite intact, as if no harm had befallen it.

"So how is all this possible?" Eenk finally asked. "How did I end up here? How did the seal and... Foof, is it...? get here days before I did? How is it that the boat, or whatever it is, now lies before us in fine shape, instead of in so many pieces at the bottom of the gorge?"

"I will be glad to answer all of your questions," Ozma replied, "but there is still one person who has yet to arrive, to hear the full explanation, as well."

At once, all present in the room heard footsteps approaching from the hallway, and presently, a stout fellow appeared in the doorway.

Neither Eenk, nor Foof, nor the seal recognized him, but Ozma greeted him with a smile of recognition, which the stranger returned. It must be noted that just as the three adventurers found him unfamiliar, he could not recall ever having met any of them, either. Instead, it was catching sight of the boat that ignited a strong spark of recognition for him.

He heavily marched to the vehicle and began to examine it with much interest. The three adventurers watched this, intently. All present noticed that three of the vehicle's wheels read "A circle of fifths," while the remaining wheel read "A tritone."

Reading this odd wheel, the stout stranger said to himself: "Is that so?"

Crouching close to it and grasping the metal device that was hanging from a chain around his neck, he struck the yet unexplained object against the odd wheel, and then held the device close to one of his large ears. He then struck one of the regular wheels, and listened again.

"It has, indeed," he announced, "been flatted!"

As if proud of delivering this diagnosis, he stood and addressed all those present: "This marvelous object which I have just consulted is called a 'tuning fork,' and it allows me to know the exact sonic frequency of anything at all, by how it and the object of examination differ in sound."

To the three adventurers, the stranger's second pronouncement was just as baffling as his first one had been.

"Why would anyone need such a magical device?" Eenk asked.

The robust stranger bellowed: "Magical?! You err. This fine invention of mine relies entirely upon my own skill of judgement, honed over many years of experience, to be of any use at all. Marvelous and clever though it may be, it is only an aid."

"Then why would anyone need such a... mundane... device?" Eenk inquired, editing his previous question.

"A fellow of my profession has much use for it," was the stranger's vague reply.

"And what profession might that be?" Eenk asked, growing

irritated by this string of unhelpful answers.

"Egads!" exclaimed the stranger, genuinely amazed. "Do you truly not recognize me? I am the internationally famous Quaver the musician!"

At this, Eenk and Foof were deeply startled.

Quaver continued: "I had been invited here to the Emerald City of Oz, so that I might put on several performances, but some mornings ago, when I forced myself awake in my home and sought my handy vehicle which you now see here before you, I instead found its shed empty, with the door wide open."

Ozma stepped in, to continue the explanation of events: "When the hour of his first scheduled performance was at hand, no-one could find Quaver within the Emerald City. Therefore, I sought him out in my Magic Picture, which shows me anyone or anything that I wish to see. In this way, I learned of his plight, and therefore used the power of my Magic Belt to instantly transport him here."

"If you had not intervened," Quaver cordially said to her, for he was as proud of his manners as he was of his talents, "many of my loyal fans here in the Emerald City would have been devastated by my performances being canceled, on account of my usual means of transport being fiendishly stolen from me by some culprits."

Eenk and Foof desperately wished, at that moment, to disappear into thin air, lest Quaver should learn the identity of said culprits who were right in front of him.

Noticing their anxiety, Quaver addressed them, thusly: "I already know, you rascals!"

They were then expecting a thrashing from the musician, but Quaver held his temper, in the presence of such a lady as Ozma, who gently raised her hand in a gesture of calm.

"By the time I transported Quaver here to the Emerald City," Ozma said to them, "he only had time to briefly explain to me about his missing vehicle, before he had to immediately rush off to begin the first performance. This left me alone to investigate, by means of the Magic Picture. Gazing into it, I watched Quaver's vehicle being driven toward a small village in the Gillikin country, at sunset, and took note of you two and the seal, riding in it. The next morning, I again sought out Quaver's vehicle in the Magic Picture, and witnessed Eenk taking it by himself, leaving his companions behind."

At this point in the explanation, Foof and the seal glared at Eenk.

"A Gillikin family had taken us in for the night," Foof said to Eenk, "but when we tried to find you the next morning, we barely caught the final glimpse of you as you were riding away, and you must not have heard our shouting."

"Or could it have been," added the seal, "that you simply were not listening?"

Ozma continued to Eenk: "Seeing this selfish and thoughtless act of yours, I immediately used the power of the

Magic Belt to transport Foof and the seal here, and brought them before the Magic Picture. All of us watching your progress from afar, I magically placed several annoyances and obstacles in your path, Eenk. First, there were the purple branches to pummel you, then the tall weeds to vex you, and then the broken bridge to remove the vehicle from your use."

Though Eenk was normally not one to ever feel shame or embarrassment, as he generally did not give a pin what anyone else thought of him, in this moment, a twang of some hitherto unfamiliar and disheartening emotion did come over him.

"As soon as you leapt from the vehicle and let it fall into the gorge," Ozma further explained, "I used the Magic Belt to safely transport it here to the Emerald City, as it was Quaver's property and ought not be lost or destroyed."

"And I thank you kindly, for that!" Quaver exclaimed, bowing as robustly as his voice was speaking.

"But," Ozma said to Eenk, "I had one more series of magical punishments in store for you: while you were walking upon the Yellow Brick Road during daylight, I obscured the friendly villages from your view, so that you would find no people to aid you. Even more fittingly, while you slept next to the Road at night, I confounded your direction and landmarks, so that you would walk back along the same path you had just passed, and thus ultimately make no progress. Only in this way could you be constructively punished, and finally be made to feel even the slightest bit of guilt."

"I see," Eenk simply replied.

"But now," Ozma said, "everyone may make themselves comfortable and indulge in the palace's conveniences. Tonight, after Quaver has given his final scheduled performance, we shall all meet again, for there was much purpose in your adventure to Oz."

14

A Musical Performance

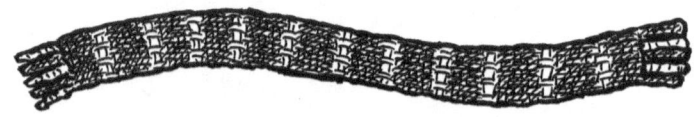

Late in the day, many citizens of the Emerald City gathered around a certain public place, in anticipation of Quaver the musician's final performance of his current tour of the city. The citizens were, of course, all clad in their "better green," which is a step up from "good green," which is the typical fashion for daily life in public.

So these citizens in their better green all applauded when Quaver the musician appeared in a small procession, which consisted of Eenk and Foof on foot, and the seal carefully driving the boat filled halfway with water, manipulating the controls with his front flippers. Quaver carried with him a box that was nearly as big as he was.

The Wonderful Wizard of Oz awaited them at the area that

was to serve as the stage, an ornate bench of marble backed by a high, curved wall, also of marble. As the musician arrived upon this place, the Wizard assembled a few large cones on stands, with the larger ends facing the citizens and pointing to every direction that the wall faced. With the utterance of a few magic words and the successful execution of several passes of his hand, the cones were rendered with a magical power that made every sound put forth at the stage spread throughout the entire Emerald City.

After a brief introduction by the Wizard, who then stepped away to mingle with the three adventurers, Quaver sat down upon the marble bench and opened the massive box that he had carried with him. From out of this box, he produced the oddest looking device, or machine, or contraption, or whatever it was, that anyone had ever seen.

How might such an object be described? It bore ivory tiles like a floor, bellows like at a blacksmith's forge, buttons like a typewriter, and switches like an electrical appliance.

Now under Quaver's control, this whatever-it-was began to move, nay, breath! as if alive, and from its lungs issued forth such a sonorous rotundity, a magically melodious music of magnificent multiplicity that had the citizens enthralled and captivated, as well as tongue-tied.

At once, Foof recognized the timbre, for it was like no other sound in the land of Oz, or anywhere else of which he knew, for that matter. But he would not dare mention this aloud, just yet, lest he be distracted from even a single moment of the show.

~~~

The performance went on for quite some time, and the sun was beginning to set, before Quaver concluded, amidst jolly cheering and merry jubilation from the citizens.

"Eenk," Foof finally said, "that music was what I heard from Quaver's hut as I happened to pass by it, one night."

"Then I understand why you kept passing," Eenk replied.

"My good fellow," the Wizard interjected, "do you mean to say that you do not find Quaver's music pleasing?"

"I do not particularly find anything pleasing," Eenk noted, "so why should this music be received differently?"

Rising from the marble bench and rejoining his procession, he regarded the pleased expressions from most of those present. Foof, having finally laid eyes upon the instrument that he had once heard in their own country, was more curious than ever about it, and sought Quaver's attention.

"That ingenious apparatus which you brought to life and bid to sing in many voices..." he inquisitively extolled, "what is it?"

"It is a mechanical contrivance of my own creation," Quaver explained, "and it is the only one of its kind in the entire world. I call it... the Quaverous Sonophone!"

"In Omaha," interjected the Wizard, "such a thing was called an accordion."

"The very idea!" the musician exclaimed, "...that even the

people of that country are familiar with my work! My reputation truly precedes me."

15

A Gift Giving

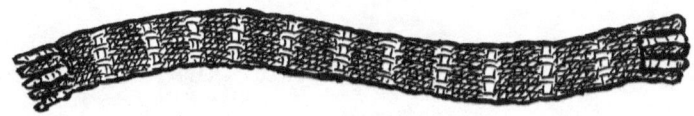

With the performance concluded, Quaver and his entire procession, which now including the Wizard, ventured into the palace to meet again with Ozma of Oz, as she had bid. The seal exited the vehicle which had conveyed him there, and was now hopping and scampering alongside the others.

By this point, Eenk was no longer willing to look at the wheels of the vehicle, for fear of discovering some new message upon them, but being so irritated by his own bafflement about the subject, he finally made the mistake of demanding an explanation from Quaver. It was a mistake, in the sense that it caused Quaver to answer.

"It makes perfect sense that if moving in one direction is a fifth," the musician said, "then moving in the opposite direction is a fourth."

"Because four comes before five, and five is after four?" Eenk inquired, wondering if the answer really was so obvious and simple.

But the musician replied: "That is not the reason!"

Eenk's confusion only deepened, the more that Quaver attempted to explain.

"It is a circle," the musician stated, drawing in the air, with his finger.

However, what he drew was a straight line.

"First, fifth, second, sixth, third, seventh," he said. "This is how the circle works in one direction. As for the other direction..."

From that point, the musician continued lecturing for another minute, as Eenk neither spoke a word of his own nor listened to any that were said to him.

"Quaver," Eenk finally interrupted, "let us never again speak to each other."

~ ~ ~

Waiting for this entourage, various important citizens were assembled in the throne room, all in their "best green," which is a step up from "better green." Seated upon the massive marble and emerald throne was Ozma, herself, who appeared even more magnificent than usual, in such splendor, and was flanked by the very famous Scarecrow on her right side, and by the very humble Uncle Henry on her left side. Both fellows regarded Quaver and his procession with much interest.

"We all offer our sincere gratitude and admiration for your performances," Ozma said to Quaver, "and we are already anticipating likewise, next year."

Quaver made a stout, courteous bow to the girlish ruler.

"Now," Ozma addressed the important citizens gathered as witness, "these three adventurers, Eenk and Foof who are neighbors of Quaver, and the seal from a river that lies on the far side of the Deadly Desert, have come to Oz in search of help, and it is our intent to honor that."

Then to the seal, Ozma said: "It is your wish to freely walk upon the land as well as you swim in the water, is it not? Furthermore, it is your wish to do so, without losing the water forever, in gaining the land, is it not?"

"That is what I wish for, more than anything," the seal replied.

At a signal from Ozma, the Wizard approached the seal and began to perform a complicated spell. He made languid, yet contorted magical gestures and chanted untranscribable magic words for several minutes, and then drew a sword as if from thin air.

With the final supernatural syllable uttered, the Wizard

brought the sword down swiftly and cleanly onto the top of the seal's head, at which point the sword vanished. All who witnessed this ritual waited with anticipation to behold what would result from it.

After a few moments, a fissure appeared upon the seal's head, and then spread down the entire length of his back, and his very skin fell off cleanly onto the marble floor.

There, appearing beneath it, was the form of a handsome young man clad in "best green." This newly appeared fellow stood up and stepped forward, completely free from the seal skin that lay on the floor in one piece. He would have looked even more dignified, if not for having such trouble maintaining his balance upon two legs.

"When you please to walk upon the land," the Wizard explained, "you may step out of your seal skin and do so as a citizen of the Emerald City. But when it pleases you to swim within the water again, you need only return to your seal skin and wear it, and at once you shall again be a seal. In this way, you may move freely between the land and the water, and vice versa."

Standing on two feet and walking, now more steadily, the seal-man was very much pleased, and bowed deeply to the Wizard, as well as to Ozma. In doing so, he nearly fell over forward, but the Wizard assisted him in not doing so.

Eenk assumed that it would next be his own turn to be helped, but instead, Ozma directed her attention to Foof, and said: "Though you, Foof, have sought the land of Oz not for the sake of receiving any boon at all, we nonetheless have three for you."

Surprised, as well as unaccustomed to receiving gifts from anyone, Foof sheepishly stepped forward.

"In your travels through the swamp," Ozma spoke, "you lost both of your galoshes, did you not?"

"I did," Foof replied, upon which point the Wizard held

up two shining, tall galoshes for Foof to behold, and then placed them upon the marble floor.

"These fine galoshes," the Wizard explained, "were made for you by the extremely talented tinsmiths under the employ of the Emperor of the Winkies, who is, himself, made of tin."

Delighted, Foof exclaimed: "Oh! They are fine, indeed! I must thank the tinsmiths, as well as their employer... er, emperor!"

But his legs naturally being so short, he could not step into the galoshes, which were as tall as the ones he had lost, but were much more attractive.

Ozma, of course, knew that Foof would be foiled by this challenge, and here is where the second boon came into play.

"During your journey here to Oz," the girlish ruler said to him, "you were several times unable to be assisted, because of the needle-sharp hairs that grow upon you, were you not?"

"I was," Foof replied. "This has been the case, most of my life, in fact."

The Wizard then held out his hands and said to Foof: "Here, my good fellow, allow me to assist you into your new galoshes."

"I would gladly accept your assistance," Foof lamented, "but it would cause you great pain to..."

Noticing a smile upon the Wizard's face, Foof stopped his speech short.

The Wizard picked Foof up and lowered him into the galoshes, and thereby Foof regained his former height, at last, while the Wizard had not experience any stinging pain or injury, whatsoever.

"While Ozma was distracting you by inquiring about your spines," the Wizard explained, "I caused them to soften, by means of a quietly cast enchantment. They are now quite harmless."

"Then it is now you, Wizard, whom I thank!" Foof exclaimed.

As joyful as Foof was, there was still one more boon to be bestowed upon him.

"While you were driving Quaver's vehicle," Ozma questioned him once more, "did you not have any proper appendages by which to manipulate the controls?"

"I did not," Foof replied. "But more importantly, I have great difficulty in picking the fruit that grows in my orchard, back home, as I have no arms."

"Please allow the Wizard to lay out your scarf upon the floor," Ozma requested.

Foof, of course, consented, and the Wizard indeed laid Foof's scarf out upon the floor, so that it was stretched out in a more-or-less straight line.

Ozma then arose from her throne, and as she did so, the very atmosphere in the room inexplicably pulsed. Silence befell all those in attendance.

She gracefully stepped toward the scarf, for the honor and pleasure of bestowing this third, greatest, and most costly boon would be hers. She held her hand out over the scarf and sprinkled a strange powder neatly upon it, from one end to the other.

At once, the scarf began to fidget about, much to Foof's astonishment.

"By means of the Powder of Life," Ozma explained, "the recipe of which is now lost, the scarf has come to life, and will henceforth be your assistant."

The Wizard carefully wrapped the scarf around Foof's neck. Placed there, the two dangling ends of the scarf acted like arms, and even saluted Ozma.

"And now it is you, your majesty, whom I thank!" Foof replied.

16

A Learned Council

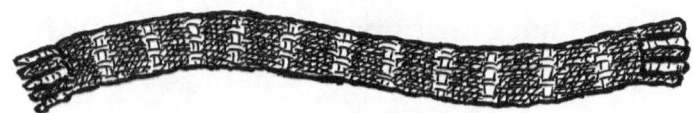

Eenk tried not to take much notice of these three impressive favors given to Foof, nor to the truly astonishing one granted to the seal. But Eenk was, in truth, bothered by the fact that it was he, himself, who had been the impetus for the adventure, yet he was seemingly forgotten at this time.

He was, of course, wrong in this assumption.

"I am told," Ozma said to him, "that you sought the land of Oz, so that you might seek advice, concerning a problem with your orchard. I now present to you: Henry, who is greatly experienced in the ways of agriculture, as well as being the uncle of a Princess of Oz; and the Scarecrow, a fellow widely renowned for his thinking brains and his sagely wisdom, who himself is no stranger to the ways of assisting fields of crops."

The scarecrow and Uncle Henry both bowed to Eenk, who only regarded them with curiosity in return.

"Please," said the Scarecrow, "explain the problem to me, and I shall wisely advise you."

Thus prompted, Eenk suppressed his natural urge to nibble upon what he thought to be hay protruding from the Scarecrow, and explained to him: "No matter what I do to the trees in my orchard, they do not bear fruit. In fact, they never have, for as long as I have tended to them."

Continuing: "The leaves are renewed every springtime. Rain falls, and dew lingers in the mornings. The soil supports an abundance of plants and earthworms. Bees buzz through the air. But still, my trees bear no fruit."

The Scarecrow thought for a minute or more, and then said: "This is an agricultural matter, and though I do have some knowledge of that genre of information, being that I am stuffed with straw and had once been employed to defend a cornfield, I must admit that trees are not my area of expertise. I therefore advise you to consult with Henry."

Unimpressed with the Scarecrow's supposed brains, Eenk then turned to Uncle Henry, who had also listened carefully to the description of the problem.

"Well," Eenk sighed, "what advice do you have?"

Eenk and Uncle Henry then began a lengthy, detailed

discussion on foliage, and soil aeration, and rainfall, and several other topics of a similar nature that would not interest the average person, so I will spare you the details.

But when the conversation was finished, even Uncle Henry, the foremost expert on agriculture in all the land of Oz, had no definitive solution to offer.

Eenk was now discouraged, more-so than ever. In fact, he was so discouraged that he did not know what to do with himself. He even doubted the worth of this entire quest, despite all the marvels that he had witnessed, along the way, and all the benefits that participants other than himself had gained.

Then, Ozma gave Eenk a gentle smile.

"Now I am sure that I understand the root of the problem," she said.

Eenk listened, in anticipation, but Ozma first addressed the Scarecrow and Henry, instead.

"I thank you excellent fellows and fine citizens," she said to them, "for though you did not know the answer, you have taught it to me."

She then looked upon Eenk, and said: "The trees in your orchard are Mellilla trees, which are to bear Mellilla fruits, which are the sweetest morsels in all the world. Yet how can even one such tree, much less an entire orchard of them, learn sweetness from a keeper who has no sweetness to teach?"

Eenk, the keeper of the Mellilla orchard, was dumbstruck.

"Therefore," Ozma continued, "this is my advice to you: return to your orchard and tell your trees how much you have missed them. Tell them that such is your care for them, that you embarked upon a dangerous quest, and stole from Quaver, and abandoned Foof and the seal, and even laid down to die upon the Yellow Brick Road... all for the sake of your trees. You have indeed suffered much hardship and exhausted yourself, for no other purpose than to give your trees what they need to thrive. It must mean, Eenk, that you feel some love for them."

~ ~ ~

It was later said, by those who bore witness to this council, that when Ozma spoke those words, Eenk trembled, ever so slightly.

Nevertheless, the council was then concluded. After Ozma, the Scarecrow, Uncle Henry, and the Wizard had delivered their parting gestures to all present, the four of them departed from the throne room. Quaver and the three newly-transformed members of his procession remained behind for some time.

17

A Chosen Itinerary

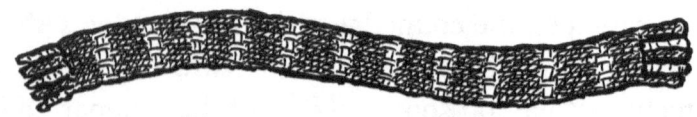

A short time later, Quaver and his procession were back outside the palace, standing... all four of them standing upon two feet... next to the vehicle with the three circles of fifths and the one tritone. Quaver examined this oddly engraved wheel, again consulting his tuning fork.

"It has indeed been flattened," Quaver stated with certainty. "It is just too bad about the Wizard's enchantment upon Foof's spines."

"Why is that?" Foof asked, unable to imagine how the enchantment could be a hindrance at all.

"Because what we need right now is something sharp to make the wheel natural again," was the musician's cryptic reply.

"I was not aware that it was unnatural," was Foof's response.

Being deep in thought, as well as not wishing to ever again hear any explanation from Quaver, Eenk paid no attention to the others.

"So what will become of us, now?" Foof wondered aloud to the group in whole.

"I, for one," the seal-man replied, "intend to walk, and walk, and then walk some more. I will walk all over this land of Oz, as well as swim all its rivers, when I have tired from walking."

"A bold plan!" exclaimed Quaver. "All that practice shall make you quite steady on your feet! It is the only way to learn. I believe that you will even master the talent. I, meanwhile, must continue on my musical tour, for I have several other countries to visit before I may return home."

This made Foof uneasy, and he said: "I wonder, then, how Eenk and I will get home."

"Yes," the musician muttered, "that is a mystery, indeed."

Foof was now greatly worried, and surely Eenk would have been, too, if he had been listening.

Regarding Foof sideways, Quaver said: "Well, I suppose that you two may return by the means you arrived, meaning in my vehicle."

This greatly relieved Foof.

The musician continued: "But I have no time to return home to our neighborhood right now, and the end of my tour will place me far from Oz, so you two will either have to accompany me for my remaining performances abroad, or remain here in the land of Oz and consider it your new home. I am henceforth your companion in earnest, if you so choose, but not your chauffeur."

"Then I think we shall travel with you," Foof decided. "Though this city and this country are marvelous, we belong with our orchards, and I am sure that Eenk is anxious to put Ozma's advice to use."

So the three of them made ready to depart, restoring Quaver's vehicle to tip-top shape.

"It goes without saying," Quaver said to his companions, anyway, "that the only true captain of this vessel... is me!"

~~~

In this way, the three neighbors: Quaver the musician, the newly very handy Foof, and Eenk the tree-tender, along with the formidable Quaverous Sonophone in tow, traveled to several other countries, lands, and kingdoms, on the musician's tour. In doing so, they had many adventures and experienced many interesting happenings, but these events would be too numerous to detail, presently, so let us just say that they are stories for other authors.

At their conclusion, the three adventurers returned to their homes.

~~~

The last anyone heard of the seal-man, he was walking to the Winkie country to see about acquiring a pair of tin hiking boots.

18

An Epilogue

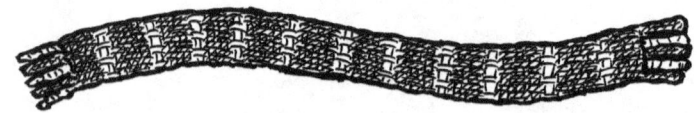

Eenk stood in his Mellilla orchard, which was still as bare of fruit and blossom as ever it had been. It was a pleasant afternoon.

First, Eenk thoroughly looked around, to be sure that no-one else was nearby. After all, Foof and Quaver had promised to pay him a friendly visit, before long.

Eenk steadied himself, and took several deep breaths.

"I, um..." he said, regarding the trees, "that is, what I mean is that..."

His speech broke off at this point, and he fidgeted and coughed, and then looked around again before trying to resume.

"Hopefully," he continued, "you trees have, er... been well, while I was away."

He paused to examine the trees, but saw no change in them.

"I should say that, um..." he started again, "that I... I... missed you..."

Having uttered this, he could speak no more. Fidgeting again, he nervously verified once again that no-one else was nearby, and then went inside his house, as if to hide.

Now being quite shut away to consider this truly novel feeling that you or I might call 'care,' he could not see that on one of the trees, there was now a small blossom that had not been there, before.

THE END

About the Author

Charles Shearer is a graduate of the Savannah College of Art and Design. He is primarily a maker of teen-plus graphic novels and all-ages illustrated prose. He has also worked as an English teacher abroad. He has lived in the American state of Georgia, the Republic of Korea, Western New York, and Colorado.

Charles's various projects in storytelling are prefaced and supplemented on his website:

https://charlesshearer.info

About "The Answer Lies in Oz"

Charles Shearer once made a fellow musician friend who introduced him to the original Oz of L. Frank Baum. Voraciously reading Baum's 14 Oz books, Charles then set about writing an Oz story of his own, as a gift for his friend. After some years of life taking its course, it dawned upon Charles that perhaps other people, as well, might enjoy *The Answer Lies in Oz*. If only he still had a copy of the manuscript!

Thankfully, he managed to salvage the story from a years-old e-mail attachment. The version of the text which is presented in this edition has been edited for general audiences and embellished for publication. Of particular note is that Charles drew nearly all of the illustrations eight years after the original writing process.

Some motifs in *The Answer Lies in Oz* had their origins in Charles's college-era comics series which has since been replaced and re-imagined by a number of more recent projects; readers of *Runaway Weer* volumes 2 and 3 might recognize the 'Ayes' which Eenk and Foof encounter in chapter 4 of this book, and vice versa.

Books Written and Illustrated
by Charles Shearer

Graphic Novels

Li'l Lynn: The Joy of Childhood and Other Myths
    Life is just fine for little Lynn Herr... until friendship and fulfillment rear their ugly heads. Will she allow them into her heart, or keep being happy, instead? This question and some others might be answered in this indeed very questionable tale of how fun it is to be utterly at the world's mercy.

Runaway Weer the Burdened: vol 1 of Runaway Weer
    Close-est Companions and best Friends since beyond the Reach of Memory, Aspynn and Lindynn face both an un-precedented Challenge that may temper them for their Lifetimes and a seething Grudge that threatens to shatter far more than just a Friendship.

Runaway Weer the Corrupted: vol 2 of Runaway Weer
    The Old is destroyed, wrecked, sundered! and what survives of Aspynn and Lindynn is made anew... and apart. Herein are recorded the deep-est Sorrow, the bloody-est Violence, and the warm-est Adoration of a Hero to Some and a Villain to Others.

Runaway Weer the Accused: vol 3 of Runaway Weer
    A weary Body, a guilty Conscience, and a troubled Mind form the thin-ly bound Pieces of she whose sordid Past pursues her across familiar Water, over un-known Land, and from within her Self. Is it Justice of Madness, that the Way to mend her Life is to end it?

The Runaway Weer Addenda
    The "Runaway Weer" Series is enriched with these Additions to the Canon, occurring during and after the three numbered Volumes. As well as Stories in a Style typical for the Series, there are also collaborative Works by Praefortis (who rose from Commandant to Governor) and Lindynn Hare of Ashwood.

Illustrated Prose

The Answer Lies in Oz

      Based upon the fantastical fourteen Oz children's books by the series' creator L. Frank Baum, Charles Shearer's "The Answer Lies in Oz" is a tale for young readers and old souls, detailing the endeavor of an utterly unsociable, exceptionally selfish ...and dutifully devoted... fellow who seeks an answer in Oz!

Li'l Lynn Tells It Herself: A Novella-zation

      A hapless child is beset upon by the grim specters of friendship and fulfillment, as entirely told and mostly illustrated by none other than herself, through the prose and pictures of this canonical complement to the original graphic novel "Li'l Lynn: The Joy of Childhood and Other Myths."

Upon the Name of Oz

      In this sequel to "The Answer Lies in Oz," a visitor of vague purpose and a native of inexplicable ability join forces in pursuit of a truth beyond mortal comprehension... and discover a miracle beyond magical explanation.

Sootwork-Mauzi

      Famous amongst the locals of sundry locales, the kind-hearted Sootwork and the hard-nosed Mauzi together run both a benevolent endeavor in the black and a pragmatic business in the red.

Brevitous Accounts of Fictitional Incidents

      Initially inflicted upon the world as a series of zines, the older entries in the "Brevitous Accounts of Fictitional Incidents" series now join forces with a number of new and heretofore unseen ones, constituting this compilation of the curious, the confounding, the exceptional, the exasperating!

      Herein we shall meet the inscrutable Buskermush family, learn the happenings of Mauzi, Yunoo, and Eenk outside of their respective stand-alone books, and witness the feats and fumbles of various other figures whether human, animal, or otherwise.

https://charlesshearer.info

Li'l Lynn

The Joy of Childhood and Other Myths

"Delightful"
"Friend"
Ashley

Our ~~Hero~~ Hero

THE TOWERING COLOSSUS

A Graphic Novel
— *about* kids but not exactly *for* them —

Written and Pictured by Charles Shearer

The original graphic novel...

...and its canonical complement

LI'L LYNN
Tells It Herself

A Novella-zation of the Graphic Novel
Li'l Lynn: The Joy of Childhood and Other Myths

Also by Charles Shearer

Graphic Novel Series

THE
ARCANE·APOCRYPHA

makes ready to receive you...

In the pages which conclude this tome,
you are offered an early excerpt
from Charles Shearer's subsequent Oz book:

UPON THE NAME of OZ

There were fine houses of squarish shape, all in a row, with ample yards between them. The countryside facing outward from all of the doors and windows was as splendid as anyone could wish nature to be. It might be mentioned that all of these openings were built into the fronts of the houses, and that as long as no-one peeked behind these cozy dwellings to observe what was in back of them, beyond the sheer drop over the edge of the cliff, there was no unseemly scenery to be seen.

To the local inhabitants, who were born and raised in this part of the world, the horrible wasteland that stretched out behind their comfortable homes might as well have been a great big invisible Nothing. In a way, that is indeed what it was, for No Thing At All was the only thing that happened in it. The gray expanse of sand and rocks, reaching beyond the horizon, was as still and barren as it ever was, on this day that, thus far, had been entirely unremarkable.

Inside one of the dwellings mentioned shortly ago, little Yunoo was concentrating ferociously upon her work. Though she had produced some half-decent wares in this workshop, to-day did not seem to be working out. Neither had a great many other days, as of late. She was only an Apprentice, after all. Her father, the Master of his craft, was indeed as talented and experienced as his title suggested. As this masterful father figure sat at his workstation, he made his own task look easy. It really was not, of course, but this is how masters work. His daughter, meanwhile, was succeeding only in demonstrating that her apprenticeship was simply not very promising.

Dispelling her intense focus and finally relaxing, little Yunoo admitted defeat.

"I can't think of anything else," she said.

Her father, being as masterful as he was, managed to keep his own work intact, despite having to dedicate half of his attention toward counseling his daughter.

"They'll see right through it," he advised, "if you don't fill in the details."

Yunoo sighed: "This one wasn't very good, anyway. I'd rather just start over again from the utter start, later."

She stood up and paced around for a little while. Though young, she took her job seriously and was upset by such failures. In times like this, her thoughts were so jumbled and confused that she could not pick just one at a time to explore, thus she felt lost.

"May I get found?" she asked.

Her father waved good-bye to her, and she walked out through the front door. What would have met her gaze, had she been looking ahead, would have been the rolling hills of soft grass and the leafy trees that any of her neighbors might be seeing from their own homes, at that very moment. But Yunoo, being in one of her fits of jumbled thoughts, turned away from this picturesque vista and walked around to the back of the house.

There it was: the Nothing, the Sameness, the Stillness. Every rock and grain of sand, in the same place where it was yesterday, and perhaps every yesterday before then. To the other locals, this cliffside was the Edge of the World, where everything stopped, and there was not anything beyond it. But to Yunoo, there was a kind of reassurance and calmness in looking upon this desert; it helped her thoughts to settle.

That is what would have happened, had this been a normal day.

As her thoughts began to settle, a new one, entirely unexpected and unprecedented, entered her mind, throwing the entire procedure into disorder. That thought was: 'Something's moving out there.'

Then another: 'No, I must have imagined it.'

And then one more, before she simply did not know what to think anymore: 'Is that... a person?'

Yunoo spent the next minute in utter confusion, trying to understand the impossible scenario that seemed to be occurring. Of course, none of her neighbors would also be witnessing this, for no-one but Yunoo ever looked out upon the gray desert.

The Master was working, as usual, when his little daughter Yunoo came back into the house. Still keeping just enough attention on his work, he regarded Yunoo's bizarre mood with curiosity. This was not typical. The girl was evidently trying to think of what to say.

"You were gone awhile," he remarked, bringing his work to a stopping point, "but didn't find yourself?"

Almost not hearing the question, the girl's lack of answer was, itself, answer enough. Glancing at the shelves over her worktable, an "Oh!" escaped her lips as an idea came to her.

"I wish I didn't have to waste one," she said, sorting through the little corked bottles on her shelf, "but it just can't be helped, poppa!"

"Waste!?" the Master exclaimed. "They're made to be used! Doesn't sound like a waste, to me. Try one out, and let me see how your skills are coming along."

The girl selected a bottle, and uncorking it, poured the unseen contents from it into the palm of her hand. An observer of this scene would have noticed some kind of Something in her hand, though it did not exactly have any definitive form or color. The girl then patted it somewhat roughly upon the side of her head, as if slapping some sense into herself.

From her mouth then poured a sentence that, though spoken in Yunoo's voice, had a volition of its own and came out in one exhaustingly long breath, which you are welcomed to imitate: "I am afraid that such is my distraction that I am in need of taking a rather long walk that might cause me to be gone for perhaps several hours during which time you should not worry about me or look for me."

Then silence befell the house. It was almost as awkward as what Yunoo had just spoken. The girl looked blankly at her father, expecting the worst.

The Master furrowed his brow and stroked his beard for a few moments, which was enough time for him to think of such a quantity of words that, if he had wished it, could be masterfully crafted into several exquisite paragraphs in critique of his daughter's utterance. But he was a man who was in the habit of thinking much more than speaking, rather than the other way around, which means that he was quite a 'thoughtful' fellow instead of an overly 'talkative' one. That is to say that for every one word he might declare aloud, there were a number of others which he kept either completely unspoken or else just barely audible.

He muttered to himself at such a low volume that what little sound did escape through the fingers of his hand and the hairs of his beard was in no danger of being deciphered as anything more than an indistinct hum. If Yunoo had been able to meaningfully hear her father's discreet evaluation, it would have been:

"That one was really not convincing at all. Exceptionally unnatural and flimsy. Where has my teaching gone wrong? Am I failing as a father?"

The longer that this muttering proceeded, the more that Yunoo winced at her father's impending appraisal; the suspense was agonizing.

Slapping his knees and then standing up, the Master's countenance lightened, and he stated in his normal voice: "But I must encourage you, Daughter Apprentice, so I'll allow it. Go on and 'take your walk.' Be back before night."

Enormously relieved, Yunoo began to run outside and would have left the house behind at that very moment, if not for realizing that the empty bottle and its cork were still in her hands. Briefly delaying her exit, she deposited these items onto her worktable, and began again to leave. Stopping again, she then picked a few corked bottles from her shelf, stowed them into the generous pocket on the front of the trusty orange-colored smock which she was wearing, and hurried outside.

Continued in "Upon the Name of Oz"

The page above is designated for the reader's use, as was promised.